A NOTE TO PARENTS

Reading Aloud with Your Child

Research shows that reading books aloud is the single most valuable support parents can provide in helping children learn to read.

- Be a ham! The more enthusiasm you display, the more your child will enjoy the book.
- Run your finger underneath the words as you read to signal that the print carries the story.
- Leave time for examining the illustrations more closely; encourage your child to find things in the pictures.
- Invite your youngster to join in whenever there's a repeated phrase in the text.
- Link up events in the book with similar events in your child's life.
- If your child asks a question, stop and answer it. The book can be a means to learning more about your child's thoughts.

Listening to Your Child Read Aloud

The support of your attention and praise is absolutely crucial to your child's continuing efforts to learn to read.

- If your child is learning to read and asks for a word, give it immediately so that the meaning of the story is not interrupted. DO NOT ask your child to sound out the word.
- On the other hand, if your child initiates the act of sounding out, don't intervene.
- If your child is reading along and makes what is called a miscue, listen for the sense of the miscue. If the word "road" is substituted for the word "street," for instance, no meaning is lost. Don't stop the reading for a correction.
- If the miscue makes no sense (for example, "horse" for "house"), ask your child to reread the sentence because you're not sure you understand what's just been read.
- Above all else, enjoy your child's growing command of print and make sure you give lots of praise. *You are your child's first teacher—and the most important one. Praise from you is critical for further risk-taking and learning.*

—Priscilla Lynch
Ph.D., New York University
Educational Consultant

To Mom, Linda,
and all the Golombiks
—K.B.

Text copyright © 1992 by Scholastic Inc.
Illustrations copyright © 1992 by Annie Mitra.
All rights reserved. Published by Scholastic Inc.
HELLO READER!, CARTWHEEL BOOKS and the
CARTWHEEL BOOKS logo are registered trademarks of Scholastic Inc.

Library of Congress Cataloging-in-Publication Data

Backstein, Karen.
    The blind men and the elephant / by Karen Backstein ; illustrated by Annie Mitra.
        p.   cm. — (Hello, reader!)
    "Level 3."
    Summary: A retelling of the fable from India about six blind men who each get a limited understanding of what an elephant is by feeling only one part of it.
    ISBN 0-590-45813-2
    [1. Fables.   2. Folklore—India.   3. Elephants—Folklore.]
    I. Mitra, Annie, ill.   II. Title.   III. Series.
PZ8.2.B13B1   1992
398.21'0954—dc20   91-43076
                                                                         CIP
                                                                          AC
40 39 38   9 10/0

Printed in the U.S.A.   40
First Scholastic printing, November 1992

The Blind Men and the Elephant

Retold by Karen Backstein
Illustrated by Annie Mitra

Hello Reader! — Level 3

Cartwheel
B·O·O·K·S ®

SCHOLASTIC INC.
New York Toronto London Auckland Sydney

Long ago and far away,
there lived six blind men.
Although these men could not see,
they learned about the world
in many ways.

They could hear the music of the flute
with their ears.

They could feel the softness of silk
with their fingers.

They could smell the scent of food
cooking and taste its spicy flavor.

Together they took care of their home,
and they were very happy.

Then one day, the blind men heard
some exciting news.
The prince had received a new
elephant at his palace.

The blind men had heard of elephants,
but they had never met one.
They did not know what an
elephant was like.

"Let us go to the prince's palace,"
said one of the blind men.
"Then we can find out what
the elephant is really like."

Off they went.
It was a long walk to the palace.
The blind men grew hot and thirsty.

But they did not stop.
They could not wait to touch
the elephant.

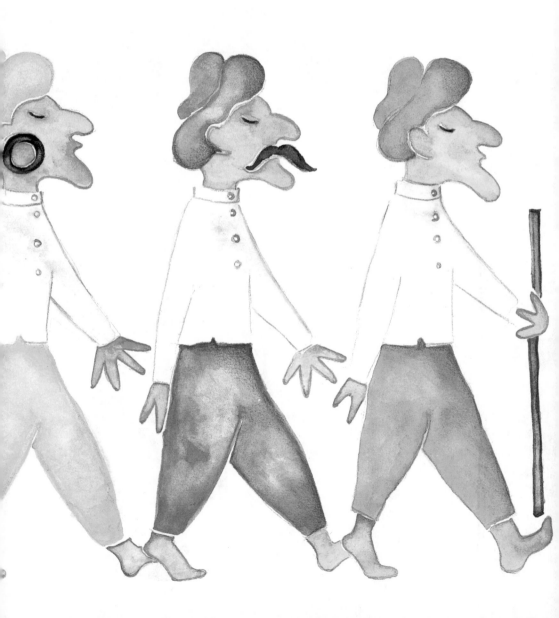

Finally they reached the palace.
A guard came to greet them.
The blind men told him why
they had come.

"Of course you may touch the
elephant," said the guard.
"I am sure the prince will not mind."

The guard led the six men
to the animal, which stood quietly
in the garden.

The first blind man touched
the elephant's side.

"It is strong and wide," he thought.
"I think an elephant is like a wall."

The second blind man touched
the elephant's long, round trunk.
"Oh, it is just like a snake!"
he decided.

The third man grabbed the
elephant's smooth ivory tusk.
"Why, an elephant is as sharp
as a spear!"

The fourth man held
the elephant's leg.
He thought it was
as round and firm as a tree.

The fifth blind man held
the elephant's ear.
The ear was very, very big.
The elephant flapped it gently.
The fifth man laughed.
"It's just like a fan!"

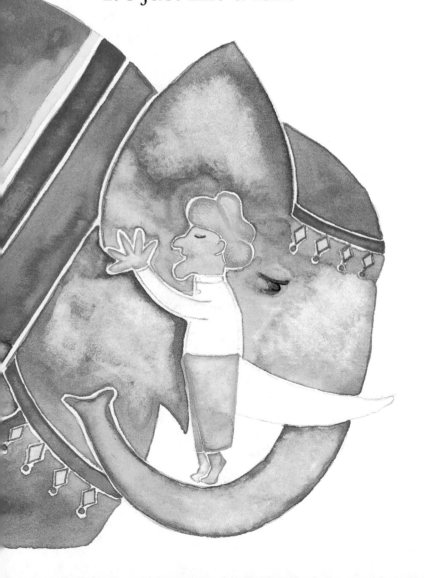

The sixth blind man touched
the animal's long, thin tail.
"An elephant is like a rope,"
he thought.

By now, it was midday.
The sun burned hot in the sky.

The guard took the six men
over to a tall, shady tree.
"Why don't you rest here?" he said.
"I will bring you some water."

While they waited, the six blind men
talked about the elephant.

"No one told me that the elephant
is like a wall," said the first man.
"A wall?" said the second man.
"Oh, no. It is like a snake."

The third man shook his head.
"An elephant is clearly like a spear."
"What?" said the fourth man.
"An elephant is like a tree."

The fifth man started to shout.
"A wall? A snake? A spear? A tree?
You are all wrong. An elephant is
like a fan."

"No! It is like a rope!" yelled
the sixth blind man.

The sound of angry voices
filled the garden.

It was the sound of the six blind men
fighting about the elephant.

"A wall!" "A snake!" "A spear!"
"A tree!" "A fan!" "A rope!"

All the noise woke the prince.
He had been taking his midday nap.
"Quiet!" he called. "I am trying
to sleep!"

"We are sorry," said the first blind man.
"But we cannot agree on what
an elephant is like. We each touched
the same animal. But to each of
us the animal is completely different."

The prince spoke gently.
"The elephant is a very large animal.
Its side is like a wall.
Its trunk is like a snake.
Its tusks are like spears.
Its legs are like trees.
Its ears are like fans.
And its tail is like a rope.

"So you are all right.
But you are all wrong, too.
For each of you touched only
one part of the animal.

To know what an elephant is
really like, you must
put all those parts together."

The blind men thought about
the prince's words. They realized
that he was very wise.

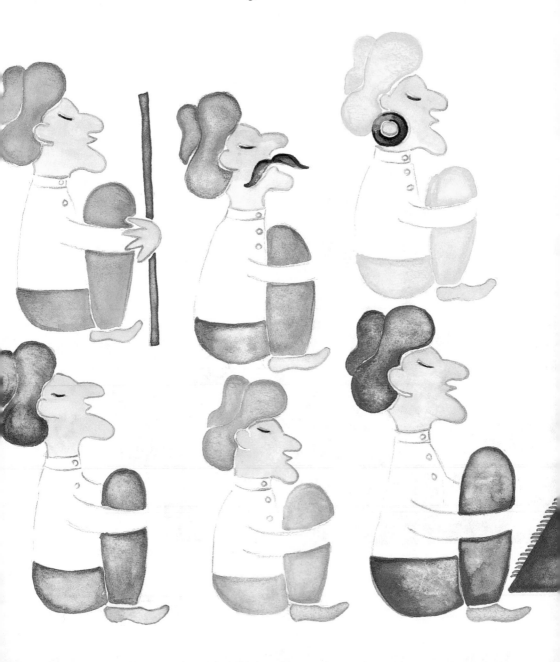

"I will tell you something else about the elephant," said the prince. "It is very good to ride on. Now you will ride on it all the way home."

So they did.

And they all agreed that was
the best part of all.